Usborne First Experiences

Contents

Moving house
Going to the dentist
The new baby
The new puppy
Going on a plane
Going to the doctor
Starting school
Going to a party
Going to hospital

Written by Anne Civardi
Illustrated by Stephen Cartwright

Reading consultant: Betty Root

There is a little yellow duck hiding on every double page, can you find it?

Moving house

The Sparks

This is the Spark family. Sam is seven and Sophie is five.
They are moving into a new house soon.

The old house

This is their old house. The Sparks sold it to Mr. and Mrs. Potts. The Potts have come to visit today.

At the new house

The next day, the Sparks go to see their new house. It needs painting before they can move in.

Two men from Cosy Carpets have arrived to put new carpets down in some of the rooms.

Packing up

It takes Mom and Dad many days to sort out and pack up all their things. Packing is hard work.

Sam makes sure his things are packed too. But Sophie would rather play than pack.

On the move

FRANK

BILL

Today is moving day. Early in the morning, the movers arrive to help the Sparks.

BESS

Bill, Frank and Bess load everything into their big truck and drive it to the new house.

Unloading the truck

Bill shows Sam and Sophie the inside of the truck. Then they all go to the new house and help unload.

Bill, Frank and Bess carry the heavy furniture into the house. Mom shows them where to put it.

Sophie's new bedroom

Dad helps Sophie get her new bedroom ready. She is very excited about the new house.

Sam's new bedroom

Sam has his own room too. He likes the new house.
Now he does not have to share a room with Sophie.

The new neighbors

In the afternoon, the Sparks meet their neighbors.
Lots of children live nearby.

MRS TOBBIT

Sophie and Sam will have new friends to play with.
Mrs. Tobbit gives Dad a big cake to welcome them.

The first night

Sophie, Sam, Mom and Dad are very tired after the move. They are fast asleep in their new home.

Going to the dentist

The Judds

DAD JUDD

MOM JUDD

JAKE JUDD

JESSIE JUDD

JASPAR

HESPER

This is the Judd family. Jake is six and Jessie is three.
Jake has a toothache so Dad calls the dentist.

Off to the dentist

After lunch Mom takes Jake to see Dr. Drake, the dentist. He is going to check Jessie's teeth as well.

In the waiting room

Jake and Jessie play in the waiting room until it is their turn to see Dr. Drake. Jaspar, the dog, plays too.

The dental nurse

Miss Day, the dental nurse, helps Dr. Drake. She takes
Jake and Jessie in to see him. Jaspar stays behind.

Dr. Drake, the dentist

The dentist sees Jake and Jessie in his office. He says Mom can come in and watch.

Jessie's turn

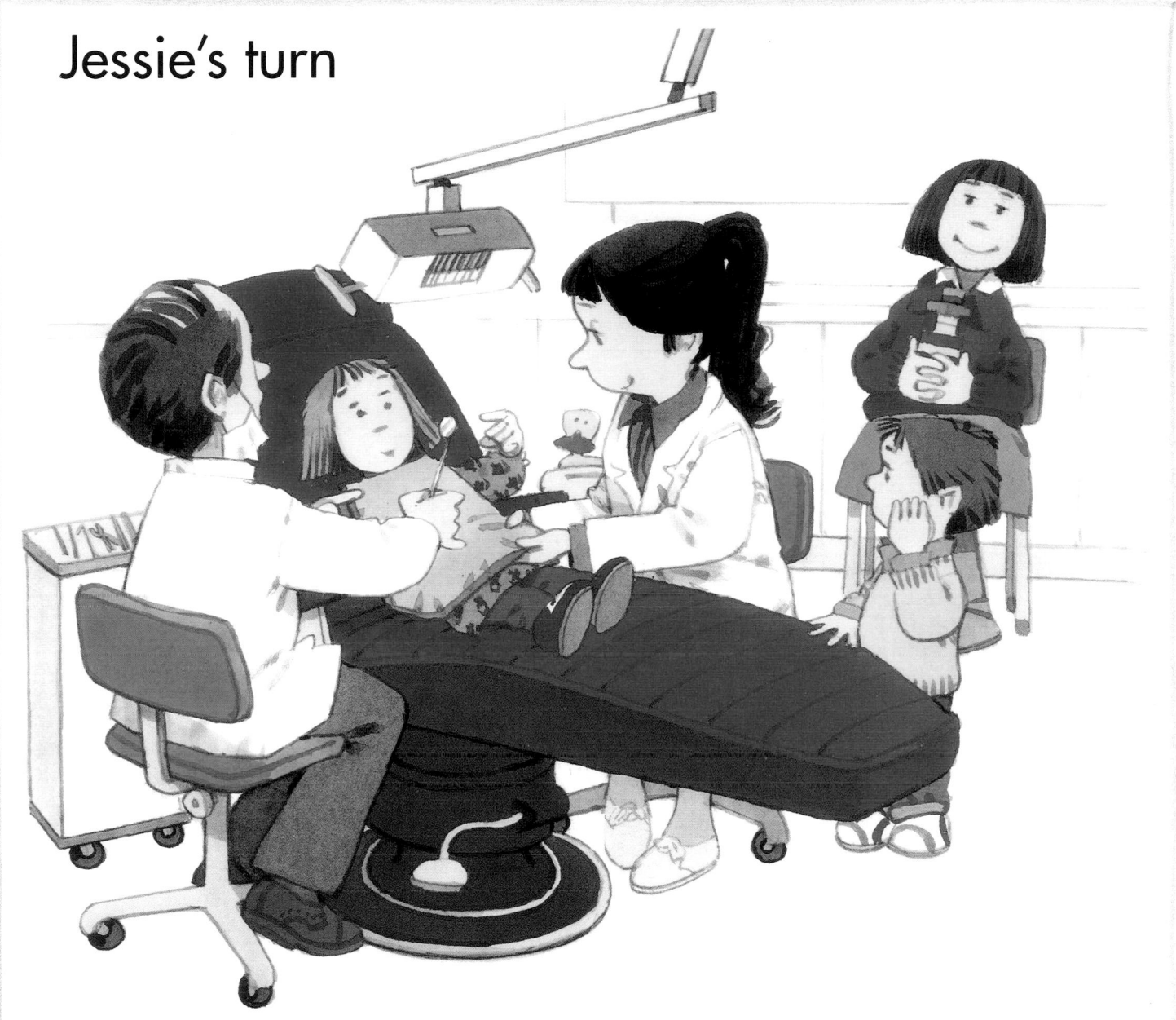

Jessie is first. She sits in a special chair that can go up and down and back and forth.

Checking Jessie's teeth

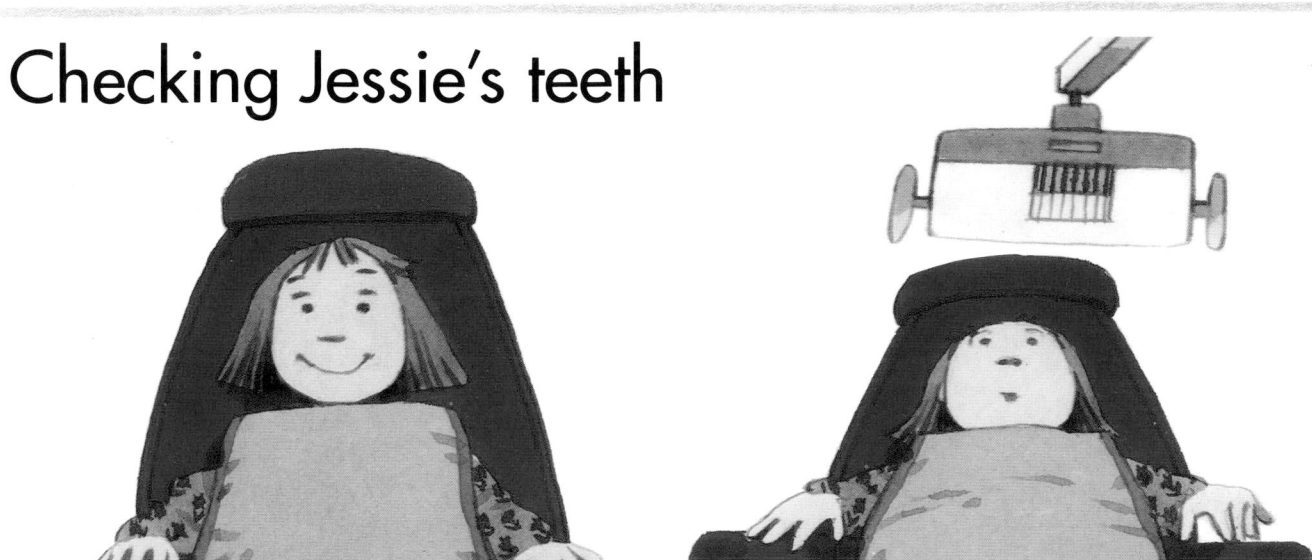

Jessie wears a bib round her neck. There is a spotlight above her which shines into her mouth.

Dr. Drake wears a mask over his mouth and nose and rubber gloves on his hands.

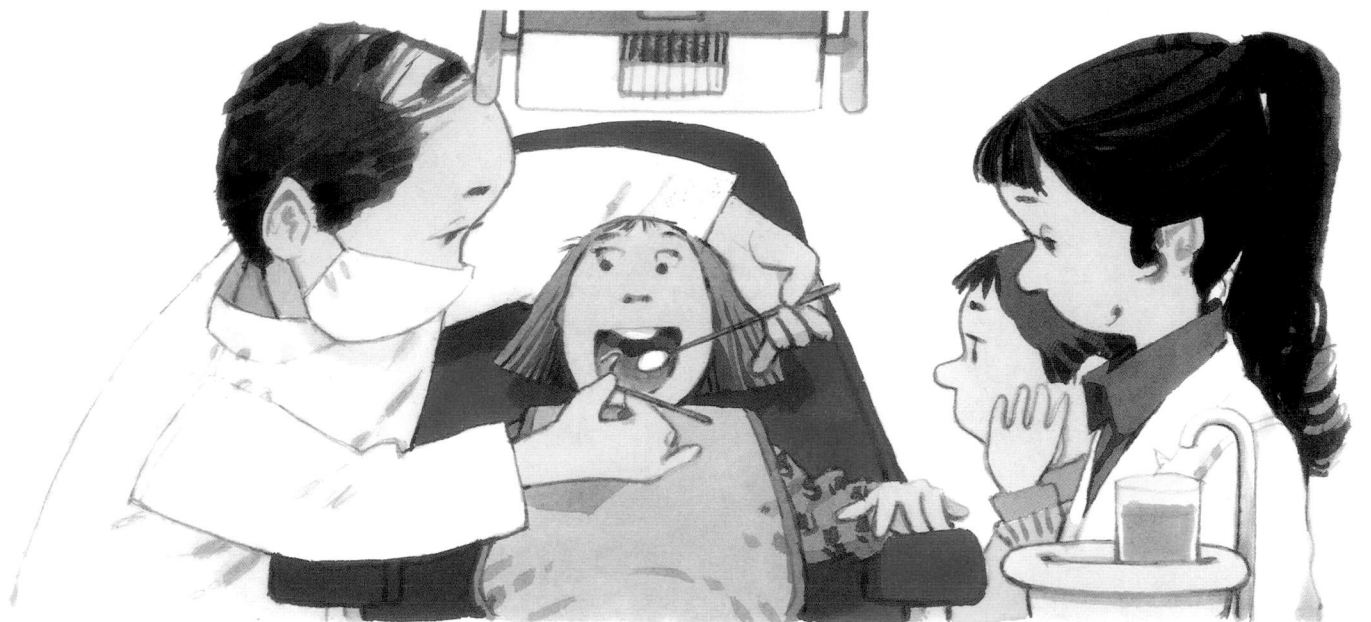

He uses a little mirror so that he can see all over her teeth and an instrument called a probe.

Dr. Drake looks at each of Jessie's teeth. Miss Day writes down notes about them.

Jessie is finished

The dentist is very pleased with Jessie. She has no holes in her teeth. Now she can rinse out her mouth.

Jake's turn

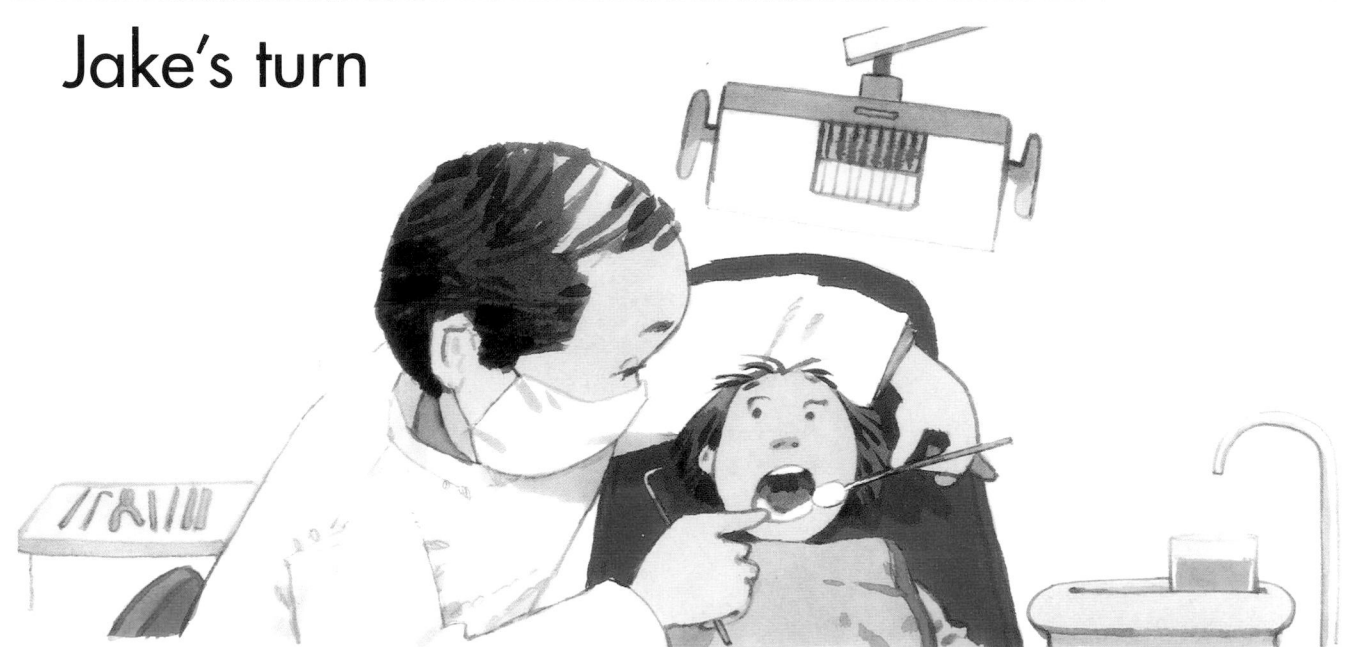

But when he checks Jake's teeth he finds a small hole in the one that aches.

Before he fills the hole, he gives Jake an injection into his gum to make it go numb. It hurts just a little.

Jake has a filling

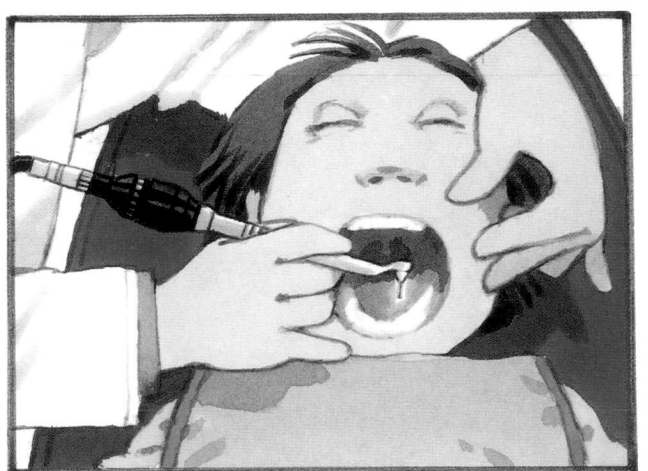 

Dr. Drake drills away the bad bit of the tooth. Miss Day keeps it dry with a special instrument.

Then she mixes the filling to put into the hole. It looks just like silver.

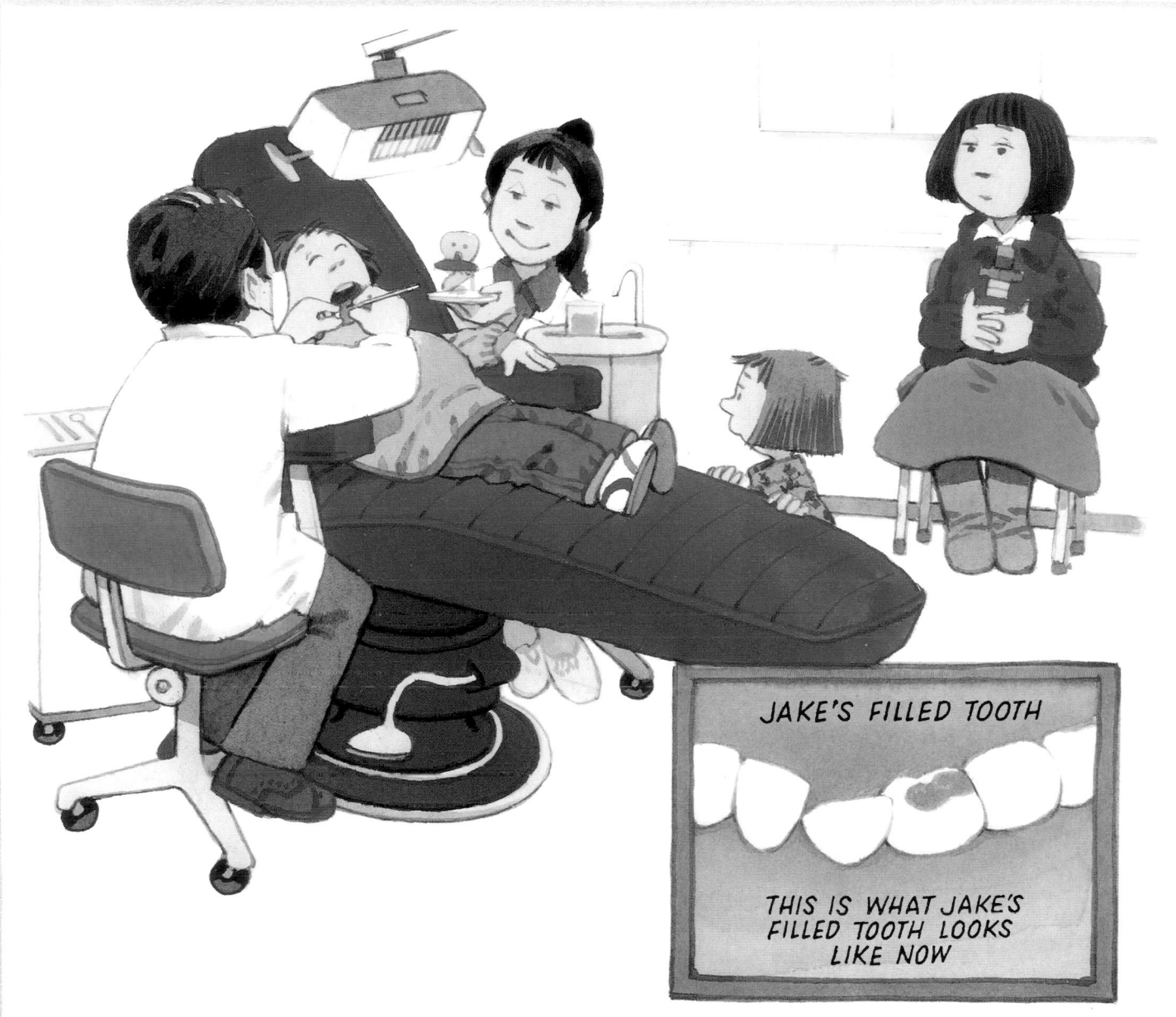

JAKE'S FILLED TOOTH

THIS IS WHAT JAKE'S FILLED TOOTH LOOKS LIKE NOW

Dr. Drake presses the filling mixture into the clean hole.
Now Jake will not have a toothache anymore.

Looking after your teeth

UNHEALTHY TEETH AND GUMS LOOK LIKE THIS

HEALTHY TEETH AND GUMS LOOK LIKE THIS

Before they go home, Dr. Drake shows Jake and Jessie what will happen if they do not clean their teeth.

GOOD FOR TEETH

BAD FOR TEETH

He says that fruits, vegetables, cheese and milk are good for teeth. But sweet, sticky things are not.

Miss Day shows them how to clean their teeth really well. This gets rid of old food which can cause holes.

Jake and Jessie must clean their front and back teeth all over every day to keep them clean and healthy.

Making an appointment

On their way out, Jake and Jessie make an appointment
to see the dentist in six months' time.

The
new baby

The Bunns

MOM BUNN

DAD BUNN

LUCY BUNN

SPOCK

TOM BUNN

BERTIE

This is the Bunn family. Lucy is five and Tom is three.
Their Mom is going to have a baby soon.

The Bunns' house

GRANNY AND GRANDPA BUNN

This is their house. Granny and Grandpa have come to look after Lucy and Tom while Mom is in the hospital.

The baby's bedroom

There is a lot to do before the baby is born. Mom and Dad are busy getting the baby's bedroom ready.

Lucy and Tom are helping too. Mom is painting their old crib for the baby to sleep in.

The baby is coming

Mom wakes up in the middle of the night. She feels the baby will be born soon.

Dad gets ready to take her to the hospital while
Grandpa calls to say Mom is on her way.

The baby is born

SUSIE BUNN

The baby has just been born. It is a girl. Mom and Dad are very happy. They will call her Susie.

NURSE CHERRY

Nurse Cherry weighs Susie to see how heavy she is and measures her to see how long she is.

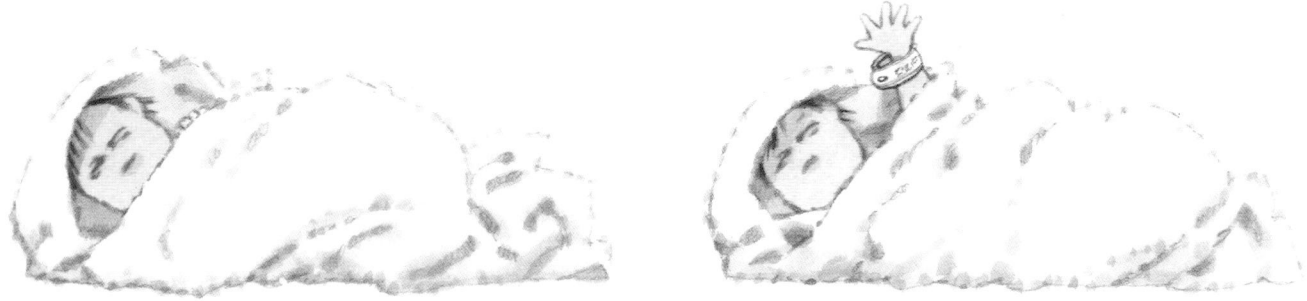

Susie is wrapped in a blanket to keep her warm. She has a name tag on her tiny wrist.

As soon as Dad gets home, he tells Lucy and Tom all about baby Susie. They are longing to see her.

Visiting the baby

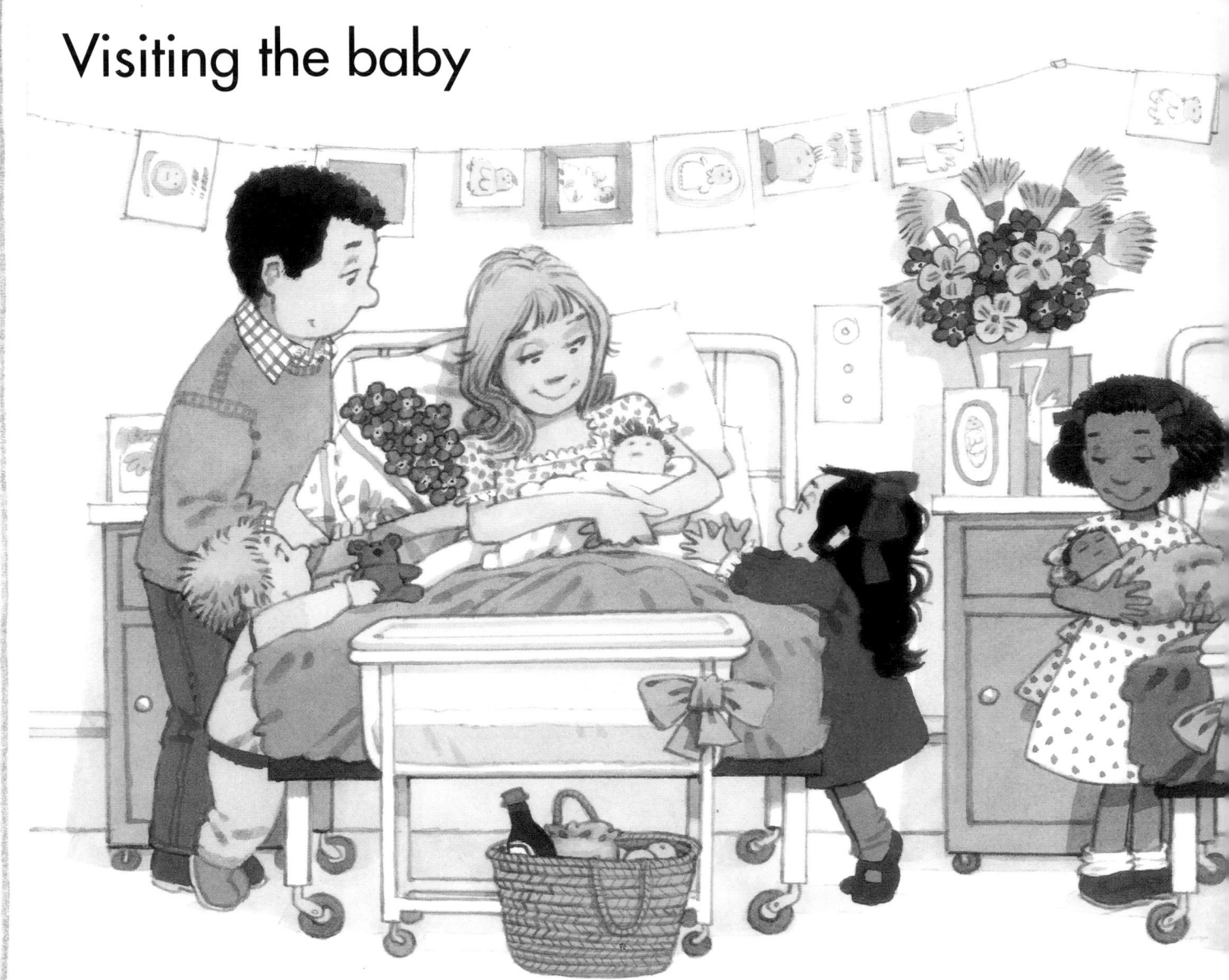

The next day, Dad takes Lucy and Tom to the hospital
to see their Mom and baby sister.

Mom is in a room with other moms. They all have new babies. Which mom has twins?

Coming home

After a few days, Dad brings Mom and Susie home.
Everyone is excited and wants to hold the baby.

Susie is very sleepy. Mom is tired too. She will need a lot of help from Lucy, Tom and Dad.

Feeding Susie

When Susie is hungry, Mom feeds her with milk. Susie will need lots of feedings each day.

Bathing Susie

Now it is time for Susie's bath. Lucy loves to help Dad wash and dry her.

Going out

Mom and Dad, Lucy and Tom take Susie for a walk.
They are all very pleased with the new baby.

The
new puppy

The Applebys

This is the Appleby family. Ollie and Amber are very excited. They are going to get their new puppy.

Hazel Hill's house

Dad drives them to Hazel Hill's house. Eight weeks ago, her dog, Tina, had six tiny puppies.

Tina's puppies

The puppies are playing in Hazel's house.
"Which one shall we choose, Mom?" says Ollie.

Choosing a puppy

The smallest puppy runs up to the children. "I like this one best," says Ollie. "Me too," agrees Amber.

Taking Shrimp home

Ollie carries the puppy to the car. "She's so little," says Amber, "Let's call her Shrimp."

Shrimp meets Brat

When they get home, Ollie shows Shrimp her new bed. But Shrimp is more interested in Brat, the cat.

Feeding Shrimp

"I think Shrimp's hungry," says Ollie to Amber. "Let's give her some food."

Ollie and Amber give Shrimp a bowl of milk and some meat. But Shrimp is much too excited to eat.

In the yard

They take her outside into the yard. "Perhaps Shrimp wants to go potty?" says Amber.

At the vet

Later, Dad, Ollie and Amber take Shrimp to the vet.
Shrimp wants to play with the other animals.

Shrimp has a shot

The vet gives Shrimp a shot so that she will not get ill. "This won't hurt her", says the vet.

Goodnight Shrimp

After supper, Ollie puts Shrimp to bed. "Please can I sleep with her, Mom?" asks Amber. "No," says Mom.

Time for bed

Dad carries Amber upstairs. "Come on, sleepyhead," he says. "Goodnight, sleep tight, Shrimp," says Ollie.

What a mess

The next morning, Ollie and Amber run to see
Shrimp. "Oh, what a mess," cries Amber.

Training Shrimp

There is a big puddle on the floor. Mom shows it to Shrimp. "Naughty girl", she says, softly.

On a leash

Then Amber and Ollie take Shrimp for a walk. "I love our new puppy," says Amber. "Me too," agrees Ollie.

Going on a plane

The Tripps

This is the Tripp Family. Tim and Rosie are helping Mom and Dad to pack. Tomorrow they are going on vacation.

Off to the airport

The next day, Grandpa drives them to the airport. Lily is staying behind with Granny and Toto, the dog.

At the airport

At the airport, Dad puts the luggage onto a cart.
"Catch it," he shouts, as one of the bags topples over.

Checking in

"Here are the tickets," says Mom to the clerk at the check-in counter. Another clerk weighs their luggage.

Security check

Before they get on the plane, the Tripps go through a metal detector. Their bags go through an X-ray machine.

On the plane

On the plane, a stewardess shows them to their seats.
Dad puts their bags into a locker above their heads.

Ready for take-off

"Fasten your seat belts. We're about to take off," says the stewardess. "I've strapped Hippo in," says Rosie.

Taking off

The stewardess tells the passengers the safety rules. The pilot starts up the engines of the big plane.

He waits for his turn to take off. Then the plane speeds down the runway and zooms up into the air.

Lunch time

"Here's your lunch," says the stewardess to Mom.
A steward gives Dad a little bottle of wine.

In the cockpit

After lunch, Rosie and Tim go to the cockpit to meet the pilots. "Look at all those knobs," says Tim.

Landing

Before they land, Mom and Rosie go to the restroom.
Back in their seats, they listen to music on earphones.

Tim looks out of the window. "We're coming down,"
he shouts. Soon the plane lands safely on the runway.

Off the plane

At the airport, the Tripps get off the plane down some big steps. "My hat," shouts Mom, as it blows away.

Passport control

PASSPORTS

They show their passports to an officer. "Look, Dad," says Rosie, "he's putting a big stamp in yours."

Collecting the luggage

They collect their luggage when it comes off the plane.
"Here are my things," Rosie says to a porter.

Outside the airport

Mom gives the porter some money. "Taxi, taxi," shouts Dad. And off the Tripps go to start their vacation.

Going to the doctor

The Jays

This is the Jay family. Jenny has a sore throat and Jack has hurt his arm. They must go and see the doctor.

Mom phones the doctor

Mom phones Doctor Woody while Dad helps Jack to get dressed. "Ow," shouts Jack, "watch my arm, Dad."

The receptionist

At 10 o'clock, Mom takes the children to the doctor.
"I've hurt my arm," Jack says to the receptionist.

Checking the records

The receptionist looks at the Jays' medical records.
"It's time for Joey's inoculation," she reminds Mom.

In the waiting room

In the waiting room, Mom reads a book to Jenny.
Other people are waiting to see the doctor too.

Doctor Woody

Now it is the Jays' turn to see Doctor Woody. "Who shall I see first?" she says to them. "Me," says Jack.

Doctor Woody examines Jack

Doctor Woody looks at Jack's sore arm. "It's not broken," she says, "but you have a nasty bruise, Jack."

Jack's sling

She puts Jack's arm in a sling. "Just wear that for a few days," she tells him. "It will get better soon."

Doctor Woody checks Jenny

Doctor Woody checks Jenny next. First she looks down her throat with a flashlight. "It's very red," she says.

Then she examines Jenny's ears with a special instrument. "Your ears are fine," she tells Jenny.

The doctor listens to Jenny's chest with a stethoscope. "Breathe in and out deeply, Jenny," she says, gently.

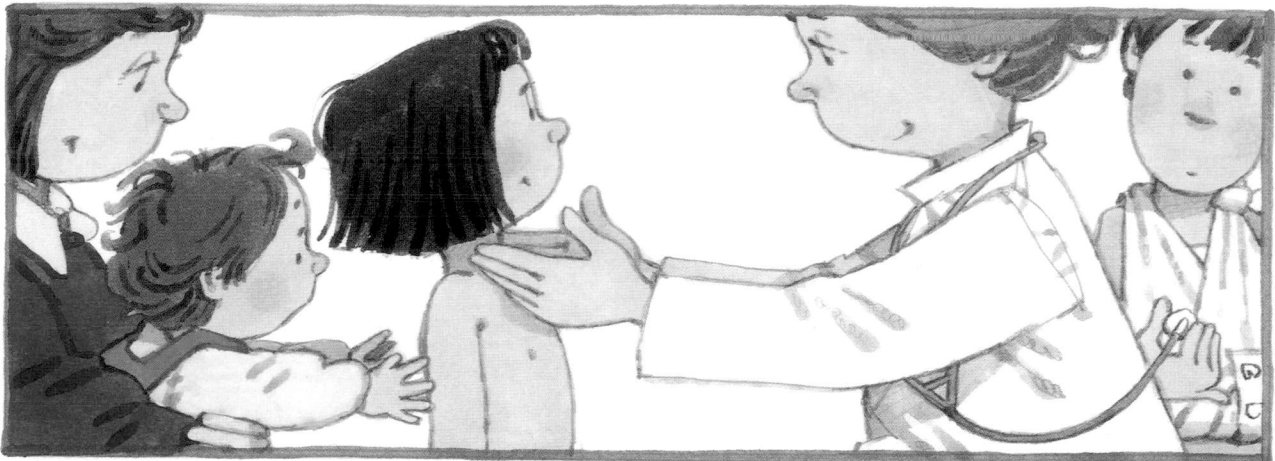

She feels Jenny's neck to see if her glands are swollen. "You have a slight infection," she tells Jenny.

A prescription for Jenny

"Jenny needs some medicine," Doctor Woody tells Mom. Then she writes out a prescription.

Joey's inoculation

Now Joey has his inoculation. Doctor Woody gives him an injection in his arm. It hurts just a little.

To stop Joey from getting polio, she gives him vaccine on a sugar lump. Then she says goodbye to the Jays.

At the pharmacist

Mom stops at the pharmacist. She gives the pharmacist the prescription and he gives her some medicine.

Jenny goes to bed

At home, Mom puts Jenny to bed and gives her a
spoonful of medicine. "You'll be better soon," she says.

Dad comes home

Later, Dad comes home from work. "Look at my sling, Dad," says Jack. "We've all been to the doctor."

Going to school

The Peaches

MOM PEACH

DAD PEACH

POLLY PEACH

PONG

PING

PERCY PEACH

SIDNEY THE GERBIL

DUSTY

This is the Peach family. Percy and Polly are twins.
Tomorrow they are going to school for the first time.

The Peaches' apartment

MILLIE MARSH

The Peaches live in an apartment above the Marsh family.
Millie Marsh is going to the same school as the twins.

Getting ready

At 8 o'clock, Mom and Dad wake Percy and Polly. It is time for them to get up and get dressed.

After breakfast, the twins put on their shoes and coats.
Millie is ready to go to school with them.

At school

MRS TODD

At first, Polly is a bit shy at school. Mrs. Todd, the teacher, says Mom can stay with her for a while.

Dad hangs Percy's coat on his own special hook. What has Percy brought with him to school?

In the classroom

There are a lot of things to do in the classroom, such as painting, drawing, reading and dressing up.

Some children make things out of paper, others make things with clay. What are Percy and Polly doing?

Making things

MR. JOLLY

MISS BERRY

Two of the teachers help the children make tiny washing lines full of clothes to take home.

Singing with Miss Dot

Miss Dot, the music teacher, teaches them to sing songs and to play all kinds of instruments.

Break time

At 11 o'clock, everyone has a drink and a cookie. Percy and Polly are both very thirsty.

Story time

Mrs. Todd reads the children a story about a big tiger called Stripes. What is Percy up to now?

In the play ground

Before they go home, the children go outside to play.
There are lots of toys in the playground.

Polly loves going down the slide. Percy likes to play in the sand. What has Millie found?

Going home

It is time to go home. The twins have had a happy day at school. They have made lots of new friends.

Going to
a party

The Dunns

MERRY

DAD DUNN

MOM DUNN

NELLIE DUNN

NED DUNN

HARVEY

This is the Dunn family. Nellie is five and Ned is three.
Ned has a puppy called Harvey.

The invitation

PETE

Pete, the mailman, gives Nellie a big letter. It is an invitation to Larry Lamb's party on Saturday.

Making monster costumes

Larry is having a costume party. He wants all his friends to come dressed up as fierce monsters.

GRANDPA DUNN

GRANNY DUNN

Granny Dunn helps Mom and Dad make two monster costumes. But Grandpa is being a bit of a nuisance.

Choosing a present

Mom takes Nellie and Ned to the toy store to choose a present for Larry. Nellie wants to buy him this robot.

Ready to go

On Saturday Ned and Nellie get dressed in their costumes. They are ready to go to the party.

The monster party

Nellie gives Larry his present. He is six years old today.
Ned thinks it is fun to frighten the cat.

Lots of other monsters have already arrived. They all try to guess who is wearing each mask.

Opening the presents

All Larry's friends have brought him a present. He is very pleased with the robot from Nellie and Ned.

Mom Lamb writes a list of who gave him each present.
He has lots of thank-you letters to write tomorrow.

The birthday cake

At last it is time for cake. Mom and Granny Lamb have made all sorts of delicious things to eat.

Larry has a chocolate birthday cake with a ghost on the top. Can he blow out all his candles at once?

Party games

After they eat there are lots of games to play. It is Nellie's turn to pin the tail on the pig.

Prizegiving

Ned wins first prize for the best costume. All the other monsters win prizes as well.

Going home

The party is over. Mom Lamb gives Nellie and Ned a bag of little presents to take home.

Going to
the hospital

The Bells

This is the Bell family. Ben is six and Bess is three.
Ben is not feeling very well. He has an earache.

Doctor Small

The next day Mom takes Ben to see Dr. Small. He says
that Ben needs to have an operation on his sore ear.

In the hospital

Ben goes to the hospital for his operation.
There are lots of other children in the ward.

Mom helps Ben get ready for bed and unpack his suitcase. Nurse Potter helps him too.

Nurse Potter

NURSE POTTER

Nurse Potter tucks Ben in bed. She takes his temperature and pulse to make sure they are normal.

Then she checks his blood pressure with a special machine. She writes down the results on Ben's chart.

Dr. Hart, the surgeon

Dr. Hart, the surgeon, will operate on Ben's sore ear.
She comes in to see him and tells him all about it.

Before the operation

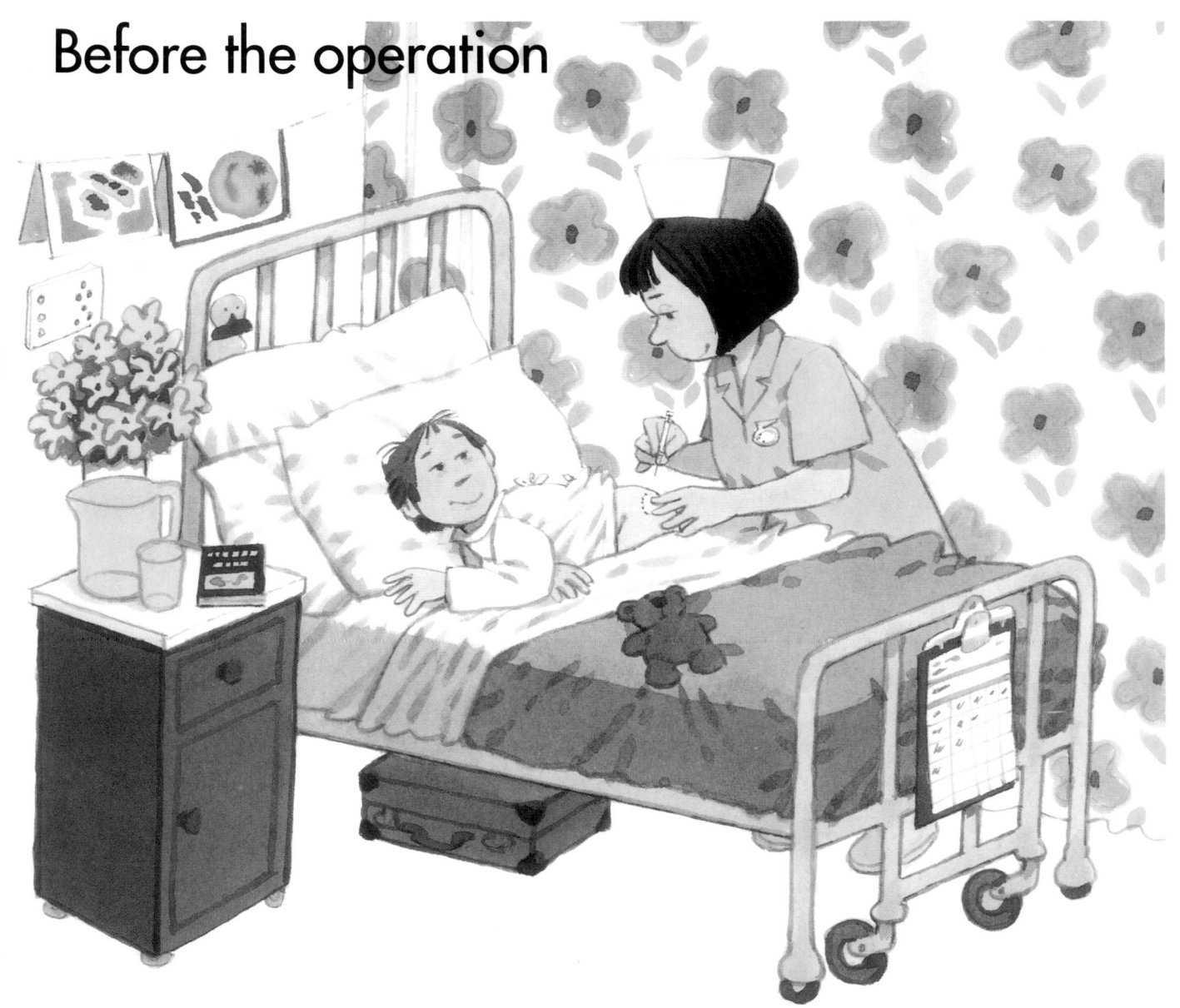

Nurse Potter gives Ben an injection to make him feel nice and sleepy before he has his operation.

Bob, the orderly

Bob, the orderly, helps Ben onto a cart. Then he wheels him down to the operating room.

Putting Ben to sleep

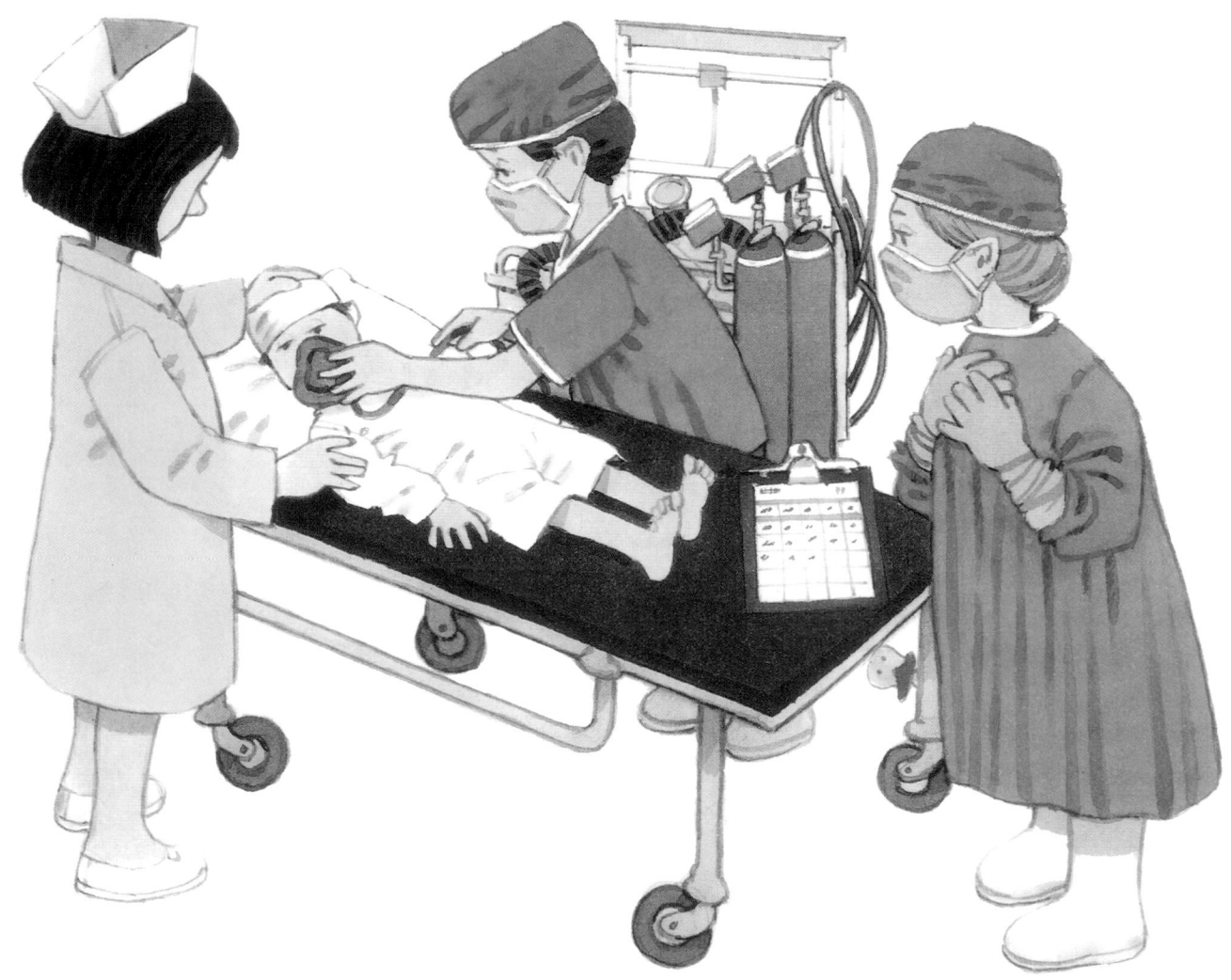

Before the operation Ben breathes in some gas. He will sleep soundly while Dr. Hart operates on his ear.

Back in the ward

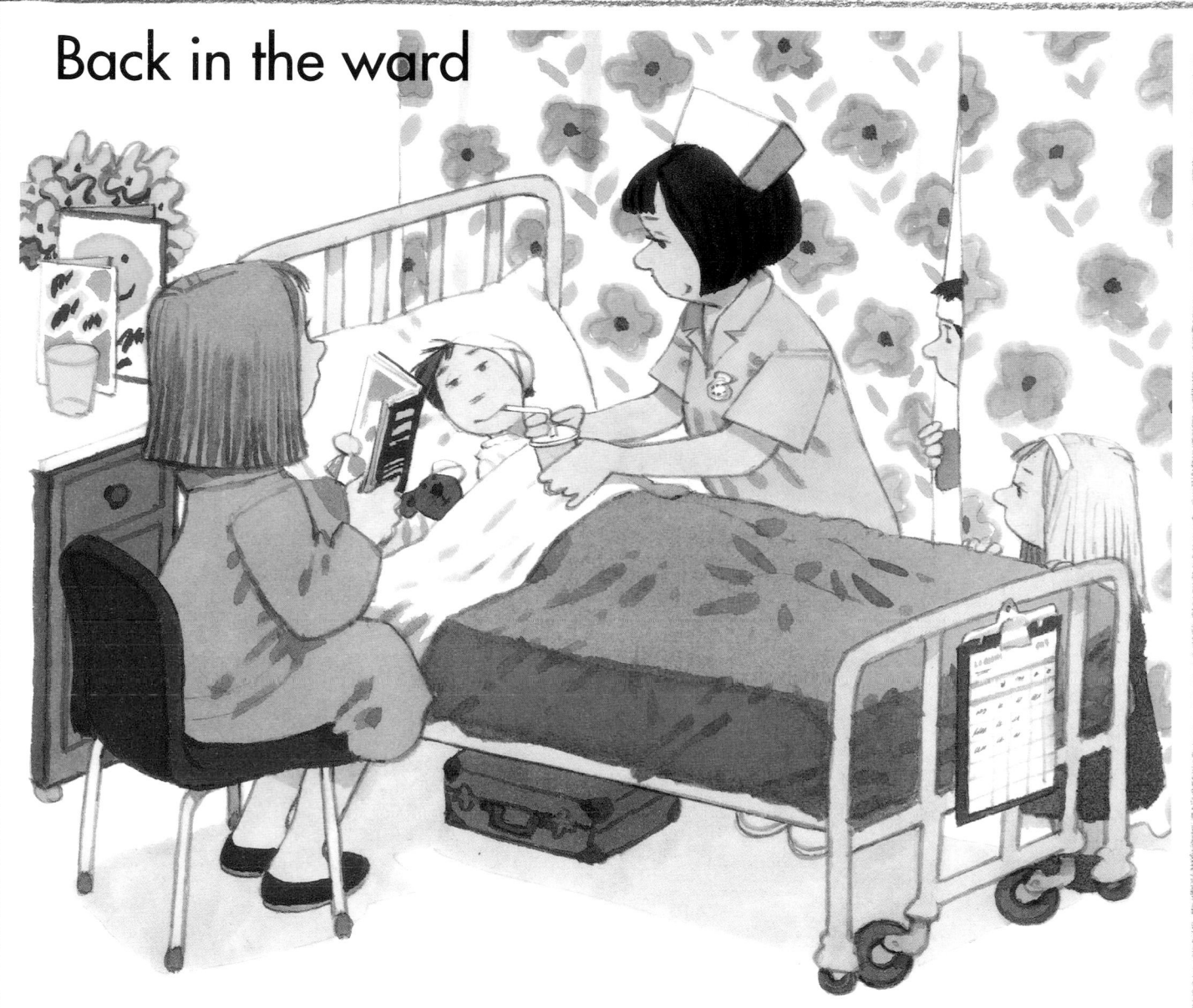

When it is over, Ben is taken back to his bed.
He is still sleepy but his ear is much better.

Feeling better

The next morning Ben feels even better. He can get out of bed now and play with his new friends.

Lunchtime

Ben eats lots of lunch. He is very hungry because he did not eat anything on the day of his operation.

Visiting time

After lunch Mom, Dad, Granny and Bess come to see
Ben. Ben shows Dad his ear. He is very proud of it.

Granny has brought Ben a new car for being so brave.
The other children have visitors too.

Going home

The next day Ben is ready to go home. His earache has gone. He says goodbye to Nurse Potter and Dr. Hart.

First published in 1995 by Usborne Publishing Ltd, Usborne House, Saffron Hill, London EC1N 8RT, England.
Copyright © 1995, 1992, 1985 Usborne Publishing Ltd. First published in America in March 1996